JACK JONES

THE PIRATE TREASURE

ZANDER BINGHAM

GREEN RHINO
MEDIA

www.greenrhinomedia.com

First Printing: September 2018

Green Rhino Media LLC
228 Park Ave S #15958
New York, NY 10003-1502
United States of America

www.jackjonesclub.com

ISBN 978-1-949247-00-8 *(Paperback - US)*

ISBN 978-1-949247-03-9 *(Paperback - UK/AU)*
ISBN 978-1-949247-06-0 *(eBook - US)*
ISBN 978-1-949247-09-1 *(eBook - UK/AU)*

Library of Congress Control Number: 2018954293

DEDICATION

This book is dedicated to my two
adventurous sons, Xavier and Greyson.
May your minds always be open.
Never stop learning and be forever curious.
Explore everywhere and
everything you can.

CONTENTS

ACKNOWLEDGMENTS

To my incredible wife, Diana, you are amazing. Thank-you for your help in bringing Jack Jones to life.

To my eldest son, Xavier, I could not have asked for a better audience to listen to the countless drafts of Jack's adventures. Your ideas, questions and input were invaluable.

To Kris, Allan, Felix and Gina, without your encouragement and support, this journey would simply not have been possible.

To Andrea, your illustrations brought us into Jack's world and enabled us to fully engage in the story and connect with the characters.

To Claire, your time and devotion, constructive feedback, attention to detail and real-world factoids helped maintain believability in an otherwise made-up story.

To friends and family members who have stuck by me in this new writing venture, please enjoy what your support has helped create.

CHAPTER ONE

The cloud-filled sky was gray. The strong wind blew sea-spray across the faces of Jack, Emma and Albert as they walked together along the wet, black sand of the rugged coast.

"Whose idea was it to go down to the beach in this weather?" Jack joked as he popped up the collar of his lucky jacket, so it was close around his neck and chin.

"Don't look at me," Albert shrugged, "it's a cold winter's day, I'd be much happier inside by the fire playing some games and drinking hot cocoa, not freezing out here like this!"

Emma sighed, "Oh, come on boys, it's not *that* cold – and you never know what a storm like this can wash up onto the beach."

Jack remembered when they had found a part of a rocket ship that had fallen into the ocean and washed up on the shore. Their photo was put in the local paper and it felt pretty cool to be famous for a few days.

Emma looked in the direction they'd been heading, her hair blowing wildly in the wind, then back at her bigger brother, Jack, and his best friend, Albert.

"Just a bit further, I promise... then we'll go home."

Jack looked down at the sand and kicked a pile of seaweed that had washed up, seeing if anything interesting was tangled up in it.

There wasn't.

"Alright, we'll go as far as those rocks up the beach and then head back home."

"Yay! You're the best, JJ," Emma giggled and began skipping happily along the shoreline.

"Come on Albert, we'd better try to keep up with her," said Jack.

"I'm just glad that next week we'll be on a hot, sandy beach in tropical paradise," replied Albert.

"Yeah, I can't wait either – sun, sand, surf – we're going to have an awesome time!"

4

The boys' conversation was interrupted by an excited shriek from Emma. They both looked up and saw her running back towards them, holding something in her hand.

"Jack! Albert! Look what I've found!" she yelled.

Albert smirked "Oh boy, here we go."

Jack laughed, "Yeah, I wonder what it is... come on, let's go and see."

With that, both boys started running toward Emma until the three met up and she revealed her discovery.

"Look, JJ. It's a bottle, and there's something inside, it looks like paper... a message in a bottle!" Emma could hardly contain her excitement as she passed the bottle to Jack.

Jack carefully held the bottle up close to his face, wiping away some of the muck with his thumb to see inside more clearly.

The first thing he noticed was just how *much* grime there was on it. Even a few barnacles had attached themselves to the outside of the bottle.

"Wow, this looks *old*, like it's been floating around for a very long time. And you're right Em, that does look like rolled-up paper in there," Jack observed, as he turned the bottle.

Albert reached his hand out, "Let me take a look?"

Jack passed him the bottle, "Sure, what do you make of it?"

"Where do you suppose it came from?" Emma asked inquisitively.

Albert cocked his head to one side, rotating the bottle and examining it from different angles as if doing so would reveal some clues.

"Well... I agree it is old. Looks like there is a cork in it and then wax over the top of that. Someone really wanted to make sure it would stay sealed and afloat. All this muck over the outside makes it difficult to figure out much else."

As Albert spoke he also picked at the wax. A little broke off and fell to the ground.

He continued digging into the wax seal as Jack and Emma looked on hopefully.

"Wow, how did it stay afloat for so long?" she asked.

"Well," replied Albert, "the air inside the bottle keeps it afloat, the cork keeps the air in, and the wax stops the water from breaking the cork down over time."

"Hey! Why don't we take it back to our house and work to open it in Mom and Dad's lab?" suggested Jack.

Everyone agreed. They hurried home across the cold, gray beach as the dreary weather continued to worsen.

As soon as the trio entered the house they tossed their coats, scarves and gloves over the sofa and Emma and Jack called out to their parents, "Mom, Dad, are you home yet?"

"We're in the kitchen," Mrs. Jones replied as the three ran noisily down the hall to join them.

As they entered the kitchen, the warmth from the fireplace was a welcome sensation, and the unmistakable smell of hot cocoa wafted enticingly from the stove.

"We wondered how much longer you'd be," Mr. Jones smiled at them while stirring the milky treat in the pot.

"It's good to see you all. Did you get up to anything interesting this afternoon?"

Emma held up the bottle and hurried over to her Mom. "Look what we found on the beach, it's a message in a bottle!"

"Oh, my!" Mrs. Jones replied, "Let me see!" Mrs. Jones examined the bottle while Mr. Jones poured hot cocoa for everyone, adding a few puffy marshmallows to the top of each.

"Here, this will warm you up," he said while passing out the mugs.

"That certainly seems like an interesting discovery, perhaps we should open it up in the lab and take a closer look?"

"That's exactly what we were thinking, Mr. Jones!" Albert replied, everyone chuckling at the chocolate moustache above his lip.

"Alright, what are we waiting for? Let's go and see what's inside," said Mrs. Jones, ushering everyone toward their basement laboratory.

CHAPTER TWO

Theodore and Penelope Jones were Professors of History and Archaeology at the nearby university. They often traveled to give lectures, attend seminars, and explore unique sites all around the world.

On most trips, they were fortunate to be able to take their children along with them. Since they were close friends with Albert's parents who lived next door, he was regularly able to join them as well.

Another helpful benefit of their work was the fully-featured laboratory and workshop they had in their basement.

It was equipped with all the latest technology and tools. They also had access to the most thorough academic databases available.

Once they reached the lab, the group wasted no time in setting the bottle in a tray and placing it on the large work bench in the middle of the room.

Everyone gathered around and watched as Mr. and Mrs. Jones, being diligent and professional archaeologists, firstly spent a few minutes taking some photos and completing a 3D-scan of the bottle; thoroughly documenting everything before attempting to open it.

"*Now* can we find out what's inside? I'm bursting to know what that note says!" Emma said, tapping her fingers on the bench impatiently.

"Yes, you can honey. We'll get out of your way and leave you to it. Jack's helped us many times before and knows the correct way to handle special objects like this to make sure the important elements are preserved, so please follow his instructions so there is no damage to the bottle or its contents. We'll have dinner in an hour and you can tell us all about it," Mrs. Jones replied.

"Just call us if you need any help," added Mr. Jones as they left the children to investigate their discovery.

Jack put on some special gloves, picked up the bottle and looked at the others. "Well, we could clean it all up and see what we've got…"

"Or we could just open it up and see what that note says," Emma interrupted all jittery with anticipation and excitement.

"I was hoping you'd say that!" giggled Jack. "Alright, let's carefully break this wax seal off and then see how we get that cork out."

Jack, Emma and Albert all worked together to quickly chip away at the wax seal before moving onto the cork beneath it.

The cork had become brittle with age and had to be broken up and scraped out of the bottle opening, which took a little time.

Then they used a pair of long tweezers to carefully remove the rolled-up paper from inside.

The scroll looked and smelled very old, like the letters from Jack and Emma's great grandpa that Mrs. Jones kept in the attic.

It was fastened with a small piece of twine which Jack delicately removed before slowly unfurling the letter. There were two pieces of paper rolled up together, one appeared to be a letter and the other was a map.

Their eyes lit up and the three children gasped as they placed the letter down and focused on the map.

"Could this be a treasure map?" Emma wondered aloud.

Jack placed a clear, protective sheet of glass on both sides of each piece of paper, clipping them together – like a picture frame, but one you could see through on both sides, then turned his focus to the letter.

"What does the letter say, Jack?" Emma asked as she studied the map.

Albert craned eagerly over her shoulder to get a look.

He began to examine the map, while Jack stood over the handwritten letter. The script-style writing looked authentic, like it had been written long ago.

Jack started reading it out loud.

My name is Samuel McDougal, the year is 1726 and I'm the cook aboard the Andalucia.

We're being pursued by three Spanish warships, they have been steadily gaining and they outnumber and outgun us by a wide margin.

The Spanish have been pursuing us since we took one of their galleons, the Invincible, as a prize several months ago. The galleon was loaded with gold and treasure which we hid.

I want to document the secret location of the Invincible as I fear our luck is running out, and our time may be coming to an end.

First, you must find the island shaped like a cutlass, then follow the map to reach the hidden cave.

Our crew set up obstacles along the way so only those who are clever, and brave, will locate the treasure.

These three clues will help you reach the end and free the Invincible once more.

Clue One
A total of three paths there be,
two will lead into the sea.
The middle one is the way
to save you from a fateful day.

Clue Two
No handle, no lock, nor hinges to rust.
Balance is the key, find it you must.

Clue Three
Light the wick then take cover fast
A boom and a blast will clear the path
Then ye shall have the very last laugh.

I shall seal this letter with a map in a bottle then cast overboard, trusting the sea will deliver it to those who are worthy.

Jack finished reading the letter and smiled slyly at the others.

Albert spoke first. "*1726*? That would mean that this bottle has been floating around in the ocean for hundreds of years. Is that even possible?"

Emma picked up the bottle and poked at some of the barnacles, "It sure *seems* very old. One question, guys, what is a cutlass?"

"It's a kind of pirate sword – usually short with a straight, or slightly curved blade," explained Albert.

Jack grinned, "I think we've got a mystery to solve... if we're lucky and the message is real, this could be a super cool adventure!"

"Kids, dinner's ready," called Mr. Jones from the top of the basement stairs.

The three children bounded quickly and loudly up the stairs, excited to share the news.

They discussed their find in detail over a delicious dinner of local fish and vegetables.

Mr. and Mrs. Jones suggested they contact the Head of Research at their university's library. Her name was Naomi and she was a close friend, too – she would be able to help them learn more about the Andalucia.

After dinner, everyone helped clear the table and do the dishes, then Albert headed home.

Emma took further photos and scans of the freshly opened bottle and its contents, while Jack downloaded a copy of the letter and map onto his tablet.

CHAPTER THREE

Jack, Emma and Albert woke early the next morning, excited to learn more about the mysterious letter and treasure map.

Albert knocked on the kitchen door as Jack and Emma were finishing up breakfast, and they headed down to the lab, eager to get back to the letter before going to school.

"We need to get some details over to Naomi. I'll send her a message and see what she can find out."

Jack attached a copy of the letter and map to an email and began typing as they all gathered around their discovery again.

Hi Naomi,

We found a bottle washed up on the beach yesterday, it had a note in it from Samuel McDougal aboard a pirate ship – the Andalucia.

It says it was written in 1726 while they were being chased by Spanish warships and talks about a hidden treasure.

Can you please help us figure out if this could be real or if it's just someone fooling around?

Sincerely,
Jack Jones

Although it was still cold, the storm and drizzle from the evening before had passed.

The sun shone down on the three friends as they talked on the short walk from their homes, through the quaint village, to school.

"I hope Naomi gets back to us quickly, it would be so exciting if this really *is* a treasure map!" exclaimed Emma.

"Naomi's the best. She knows everything, and she's always fast," Albert replied.

Jack smiled, "Albert's right, I'd say we'll hear back from her by the time we get home from school today."

They continued walking, then Albert piped up again, "I was thinking about it last night. The chances of a bottle floating around in the ocean for *that* long must be pretty small."

"True," Jack agreed, "but you never do know, stranger things *have* happened!"

The children arrived at school, caught up with their friends and settled into their school day as best they could.

But it was hard to concentrate, and even in their favorite classes, their minds drifted to the exciting discovery and its possibilities.

After school, Jack had band practice. He was the lead guitarist in a group called The Missing Links. He loved music and hanging out with his fellow band mates, but today was different.

After their session, he raced home quickly to see if Naomi had replied.

Sure enough, there was a message from her waiting on Jack's tablet, he read it to the others.

Greetings, Jack.

This certainly does seem like a very interesting discovery!

I've researched the information you provided and there was, in fact, a ship named the Andalucia which started out as a Spanish trade ship but was captured by pirates in 1720.

From that time, it was believed to be led by Captain Kraken who was a notable and somewhat fearsome pirate in his day.

He and his crew are believed to have stolen goods from many merchant ships in the Atlantic but were perhaps best known for their capture of a Spanish galleon (a sailing ship) called the Invincible.

It was rumored to be transporting a large amount of gold and valuables. The galleon had been separated from her well-armed escort ships during a storm, and the crew of the Andalucia took advantage of this situation. They were able to capture the ship and flee with her and the cargo.

The Spanish then chased down the Andalucia and ultimately sank her in 1726, all hands believed lost. It was a short, but heated battle on the seas around the Caribbean.

According to records of the time, neither the Spanish galleon or its cargo was ever located.

Pirate ships didn't file paperwork with official offices, so no crew list is available, however some surviving records from that time do link Captain

Kraken, Samuel McDougal (who was the son of a poet, which likely explains his excellent literacy skills!) and the Andalucia.

I couldn't find any references to a Cutlass Island. However, after some satellite map analysis of areas the Andalucia was known to sail, I believe the most likely location is in the tropical waters around a place called Forbidden Isle. It is uninhabited and local legends believe it to be cursed.

Based on all of this, I would suggest that, as unlikely as it may seem, the documents you have are authentic and could be the key to unlocking a mystery that has remained unsolved for a very long time!

Jack looked up from his tablet and was greeted with two very excited faces.

"Well, it looks like we've got some treasure hunting to do!"

Emma clapped her hands together, "We'll be in that area next week with Mom and Dad while they give their lecture. This is perfect!"

Jack looked at Albert, "What do you say pal, are you in?"

"Of course! But I'm a little worried about the local legend saying the Forbidden Isle is cursed. Let's be prepared."

"Yeah, I think we'll definitely need our wits about us on this one."

When Mr. and Mrs. Jones returned home that evening the kids filled them in on all the information Naomi had found.

They would unfortunately be too busy with their work schedule to join the children, but they contacted an old family friend who lived in the local area.

He ran a small boat charter company and agreed to escort Jack, Emma and Albert on their adventure to Forbidden Isle.

CHAPTER FOUR

The slight jolt and screech of the tires meeting the runway announced their arrival.

The swaying palm trees were a very pleasant and welcome change from the barren tree branches at home, and the warm, tropical air could be felt as they walked through the jetway into the terminal.

The afternoon was spent at the resort enjoying the many pools, slides and fun activities.

Over dinner, Mr. and Mrs. Jones reminded Jack, Emma and Albert that while their skipper would get them there and back, they would need to make sure they were properly prepared and keep them updated along the way.

Jack agreed, and they continued to talk about how exciting it would be to solve a mystery whose clues had been floating in the ocean, waiting to be discovered, for hundreds of years.

They planned to leave first thing the next morning, so everyone went to bed early that night, dreaming of adventure, pirate ships and... treasure.

It was shortly after sunrise when Jack, Emma and Albert made their way down to the docks to meet their skipper at his boat.

They each had a backpack filled with supplies and equipment; food and water, ropes, flashlights, matches, a first-aid kit, tools for cutting through any jungle vegetation, and, of course, Jack's tablet.

"Good morning, I'm Roberto!" The friendly skipper greeted them as they approached his boat.

"Hi Roberto, I'm Jack Jones. This is my best friend Albert, and my little sister, Emma."

"Welcome! You've grown so much since I last saw you! It's a beautiful morning, the sky is clear, and the seas are calm. This is my boat, *Hercules*. She may not be one of the newest boats around, but she is sturdy and reliable."

Hercules was an older-style wooden tug boat that now offered fishing and sightseeing tours.

She was indeed an older boat, but looked to be very well maintained, and the unique style added to the sense of adventure.

Roberto's face, which had been very warm and friendly, suddenly turned more serious. "Your parents told me you wish to visit Forbidden Isle. Are you sure that's where you want to go?"

Jack answered strongly, "Yes, that's definitely where we need to go – we're following clues to solve a mystery."

Roberto smiled, "Ah, you're treasure hunters, perhaps?"

"We hope so. We found a message in a bottle, with a map!" Emma added.

"Well, I have to tell you, when I was a boy, I remember hearing a lot of stories about people traveling to Forbidden Isle in search of treasure. But I never heard of anybody finding it. It's quite a rugged and wild place, so you'll need to take good care."

Jack looked at Albert and Emma. "I think we need to be careful and look out for each other, but it would be so cool to solve this mystery and see where the map leads. We've been on lots of hikes and explored with my parents heaps of times, so I feel comfortable and prepared for this. I'm hoping there's no snakes, but otherwise I'm in! Who's with me?"

"I know we can do this, I'm in!" said Emma.

Albert looked out to sea, pausing briefly. Then he looked at his friends, "Well, I want to make sure we get back here safe and sound, but we can't stop now that we're this close... I'm in, too!"

Roberto smiled again, "Well, you are all very brave and I know that Hercules is up to the task – climb aboard and I'll take you there!"

Once all the gear had been loaded and stowed, Roberto started the engine and cast off the lines. Hercules made a low *put-put* sound as they slowly departed the dock.

The water was a deep blue and the light breeze felt wonderful as they left the protected port and headed toward Forbidden Isle. The trip took about two hours.

As they were approaching, Jack took a moment to send a message to his parents, letting them know that they had arrived safely and would keep in touch through their expedition.

The Joneses replied quickly that they were happy to hear all was going well so far and wished them luck on their quest.

As they got closer to Forbidden Isle, they could see the terrain better. The blade of the cutlass was mainly a tall rocky mountain with dense trees surrounding the base.

"Jack, where would you like me to drop anchor?" asked Roberto.

Jack accessed the map on his tablet and pointed to the northern tip of the isle, "Up here, please, Roberto. The tip of the cutlass is where we need to start exploring."

"You're right, it does look like a cutlass," laughed Roberto as he checked the nautical charts for the area.

"Yes, the water is deep enough there, so I can anchor close by. We'll need to be careful of those rocks and I can run you ashore to this beach area in the dinghy."

"That sounds great," replied Jack as he shared the plan with Emma and Albert.

It wasn't long before Hercules was anchored, the gear loaded into the rubber dinghy and they were on their way, bouncing across the small waves toward the shore as the small engine buzzed loudly.

Roberto steered around the remains of several old wrecks in the clear waters below them. As they got closer they could also see a couple of small wooden boats that were up at the top of the beach. There were different styles of boats, all in poor condition, as if they had arrived at separate times, many years ago, but never left.

Roberto slowed the engine and lifted it out of the water as they approached the beach.

With a hiss, the dinghy slowed to a halt in the pristine, grainy-white sand.

Roberto jumped out first and tied the dinghy to a nearby tree, then helped everyone ashore along with their gear.

"Alright, I'll need to wait here and keep an eye on the boat, here is a radio so we can reach each other if anything comes up. Let's plan to meet back on this beach this afternoon at three o'clock, ok?"

Albert took the radio from Roberto and clipped it to his belt. "Thanks Roberto, we'll see you soon."

"Good luck, my young friends!"

Jack led the way off the beach and into the trees, they came across an overgrown path that was heading generally in the direction they wanted to go.

They followed it.

"It doesn't look like anyone has been here for a long time," Jack observed as they hiked through the scrub toward the tip of the cutlass, where the map began.

CHAPTER FIVE

After trekking through the trees and tall grasses for about half-an-hour, the group reached a rocky, mountainous area at the northern-most tip of the island. They gathered around to look at the map on Jack's tablet.

"According to this map, there should be an entrance around here somewhere. Let's split up and look around, just don't go too far away though... also keep in mind that the entrance may be hidden."

Emma and Albert began following the rocky wall of the mountain in opposite directions, while Jack had another idea.

He started climbing up the mountain toward a ledge he could see a short way up. As he climbed higher, he found some hand and foot holds that were hidden behind vines growing up the sides of the rocks.

It seemed to him that someone had intentionally carved them there a long time ago, which led him to believe he was on the right track. Just as Jack climbed up onto the ledge, Emma and Albert both returned to where they had started.

"Jack, what are you doing up there?" called Emma.

"Following a hunch. Did you find anything?"

"No, I came to a dead-end where the rocks jutted out into the sea."

"How about you Albert?" asked Jack.

"Nothing either I'm afraid, it gets very overgrown down that path, we'll need to cut through it if we have to go further that way."

"Alright, give me a few minutes to see what I can find up here," said Jack.

He continued moving along the ledge, searching for signs of an opening as the rock face began to jut into the sea.

He pushed against the wall trying to feel for any potential lever or handle.

Suddenly his hand disappeared into the vines.

Jack began pulling the vines away excitedly as a huge grin crept across his face. There, hidden behind the overgrown vines was an entrance to a cave in the side of the mountain.

"Jack, we can't see you, are you alright?" Albert yelled from below.

Jack stepped closer to the edge and looked back at Emma and Albert. "Yes, I'm fine... and I think I've found something! You both need to get up here!"

They worked together quickly to haul themselves, and their gear onto the ledge. The ledge was covered in overgrown vines and jungle vegetation and Jack slowly led Emma and Albert along the mountainside toward the hidden cave entrance.

As they turned a corner, Emma's foot became tangled in a vine.

She tried to wiggle it free and lost her balance. Suddenly, she slipped, and fell forward over the side of the cliff.

"Ahhhh!" she screamed as she felt a hard jolt that stopped her from tumbling into the sea below.

"Jack, grab Emma's other leg, quickly!"

Albert was following behind Emma and managed to grab her leg as he realized what was happening. Her foot was still tangled in the vine, which still clung to the mountainside. Jack knelt and grabbed Emma's other leg.

"Please help!" she wailed. She was suspended upside down as the waves crashed against the rocks below.

"We've got you, Em," Jack said bravely.

"Don't worry, Emma, try to stay calm," added Albert as the two friends worked together to pull Emma back onto the ledge.

They grabbed at her sweater, then her backpack, slowly pulling her back to safety.

The trio sat against the wall, realizing the danger they'd faced and relieved that everyone was safe.

"Whew, that was a close one!" sighed Emma.

"Are you sure you're alright, Em?" Jack was concerned for his younger sister.

"We can just radio Roberto and head back if you want?" suggested Albert.

"No way!" said Emma. "It was a close call, for sure, but what sort of adventurers would we be if we turned back now?"

Jack smiled. "Way to go, sis! This way then. Follow me."

Once they were all outside the entrance, they cut away the vines to get a better look at the cave and see how deep into the mountain it went. They took out their flashlights and made their way inside.

A short way into the cave, Jack noticed something jutting out from the wall. On closer inspection he discovered it was a torch attached to the side of the cave. Not the usual kind, more like the ones found in old medieval castles.

Jack carefully used a match to light the torch. As the flame grew, it illuminated the entire cave, making it much easier to see their surroundings.

The round cave felt a little damp and the air smelled stale.

There were cobwebs everywhere, some old crates stacked against a wall, and in another area some old barrels.

Everything was covered in dust and dirt, but Albert was quite drawn to the barrels lined up against the wall, and the smell that filled the cave.

He dusted off one of the barrels to reveal writing printed on the side.

"Gunpowder!" Albert exclaimed, "I'll bet these barrels are filled with it."

"Whoa! Well, we're definitely not the first ones to have made it this far!" added Jack.

"No, we're not. But it looks like no one has been here for a long time. I wonder what they were doing with all that gunpowder?" Albert wondered.

"Pirates used to use gunpowder, right? I'd say this is good news, it probably means we're on the right track," replied Jack with a shrug.

Emma ventured a little further into the cave. "Hey, guys, there's another one of those torches and a passageway going further in over here."

The boys followed Emma, stopping to light the next torch as they made their way deeper into the cave.

Once the area was lit up, they saw two passages along the back wall, one on each side of the cave.

"Which path should we take?" Albert asked.

Jack pulled out his tablet and swiped to view the scan of the letter.

"Remember those clues McDougal left? Perhaps one of those will help us."

He examined it before pointing to the first one:

> *A total of three paths there be,*
> *two will lead into the sea.*
> *The middle one is the way,*
> *to save you from a fateful day.*

"Hmmm... that's odd, it sounds like there are supposed to be *three* passageways, and we're supposed to take the middle one."

Albert thought about the clue while looking around the area for another entrance.

Jack looked towards the back of the cave, "Maybe it's behind this stack of crates and barrels."

Albert walked over to check it out.

"Alright, let's move these carefully – we don't want any of this gunpowder exploding, or we'll be toast."

They worked together to slowly move the crates and barrels out of the way.

Eventually a small passageway, only half as high as the other two, came into view.

"This must be the third path!" shrieked Emma.

"It's going to be a tight squeeze through there," Albert replied as he looked at the low and narrow opening in the wall.

"Well, that hole's not going to get any bigger by standing around and looking at it. I say we go!" said Jack.

He attached a flashlight to his head before crouching down and crawling in. Emma and Albert turned on their flashlights and followed Jack into the tunnel.

"We're going deeper and deeper inside the mountain," Jack observed, and they continued slowly through the cramped space.

The trio braved a variety of bizarre and fascinating creepy-crawlies, bugs and insects along the way. Jack was relieved there were no slithery snakes!

Finally, they reached a large, open space inside the mountain.

CHAPTER SIX

Jack, Emma and Albert stood and stretched as they exited the cramped tunnel space. The wider area they now found themselves in was a welcome change as they could once again stand at full height.

Using their flashlights, they located a couple more torches on the wall they had just passed through. Albert lit them both and they could now see most of the cavern around them.

The three explorers found themselves standing on a narrow ledge that jutted out from the cavern wall.

They carefully peered over the edge and saw that it was a long way down, with jagged rocks below.

They needed to figure out their next move.

Jack and Emma examined one side of the ledge while Albert peered over the other.

They saw openings further along the wall, but they were sloped, like a slide coming out of the wall heading toward the deep drop and the unwelcoming rocks beneath.

Their eyes followed the path of the slides as they looked down and shone their bright flashlights into the darkness.

"*Eeek*. Jack! are they what I think they are?" Emma gasped.

Jack nodded his head slowly, "Yeah, Em, they're skeletons."

Jack called out to Albert, "Albert, we've found something over here."

Albert had been looking down the drop-off on the other side of the ledge, "Judging by Emma's reaction, I'm guessing it's the same thing I found; there are a bunch of skeletons smashed up on the rocks down there."

"Yeah, it's the same over here, too," Jack replied, "I'd say that at some point those other passages we saw must turn into slides, and whoever goes in plummets down into the darkness... and then the rocks."

Albert nodded. "I think you're right. Good thing we had the map and found the hidden path, or we might have ended up just like them. We need to be very careful, those pirates weren't messing around trying to keep people out of here."

Emma looked up from the drop-off, "I agree. This would also explain those boats left stranded at the beach!"

"You're right Em. Let's make sure we don't end up the same way, or worse... I don't see any sign of treasure around here, I think we need to figure out a way to keep going," said Jack as he opened up the map on his tablet again.

"According to the map we need to go that way." Jack pointed into the darkness across the drop-off.

The three adventurers shone their lights in that direction. They saw another ledge and what appeared to be a doorway on the other side.

There was also an old rope and wooden bridge hanging down into the ravine.

Most of the wood was rotten or missing planks and the rope's condition didn't look much better. There were iron rings in the rocks on both sides where the bridge had been attached.

A small amount of rope was still hanging from the rings, but it looked as though it had been cut, allowing the bridge to fall and swing to the far side.

"Looks like that old bridge would have been how Samuel McDougal's crew got in and out. They must have cut the ropes when they left to make it more difficult for anyone else to get across. We'll have to find another way," said Albert as he continued looking around the area.

Jack pointed to a large boulder on the ledge opposite them, "You see that big rock over there? If I could get a rope around it, we could tie the other end to one of these iron rings and get across that way!"

"You think you can get a rope hooked around *that*?" said Emma curiously, "It's a long way."

"There's only one way to find out," laughed Jack. He pulled a long rope from his backpack and made a big lasso loop on one end.

He knelt and tied the other end to one of the iron rings, held the loop end and bunched up the slack in his other hand. "Stand back you two, time for a little cowboy action!"

Jack swung his arm with the rope loop back and forward a couple of times while aiming at the boulder.

On the third swing he let go and allowed the slack to unravel as the loop sailed through the air and landed next to the boulder.

"Oh, so close, JJ, try again!" encouraged Emma.

Jack pulled the rope back and set it up for another toss. This time the rope flew high in the air and landed just shy of the ledge.

"Aww, man," sighed Jack.

"You can do it, Jack," said Albert, supporting his friend, "Don't give up."

Jack attempted the toss a third time with no luck. He knew he could do it, he just wasn't sure how many tries it may take.

"Come on, Jack, you've got this." Emma smiled at her brother, "Give it another try. I know you can do it!"

Jack took a deep breath, swung his arm once more, and this time when he let go, the loop sailed through the air and landed directly over the boulder.

"*Bingo*!" cried Albert.

"Well done, JJ!" Emma cheered. Now we can climb across."

"Thanks," said Jack, "I guess that knot-tying practice at summer camp paid off!"

He felt glad that he didn't give up and was grateful that Albert and Emma were there to support him.

He looped the other end of the rope through one of the iron rings where the bridge was once connected and tied a knot to secure it.

"Ok, I'll go first," said Jack as he put on his climbing gloves. He clipped one end of a tether onto his belt before attaching the other end to the rope.

He very carefully lowered himself off the ledge and held tightly onto the rope with both hands.

Once he'd steadied himself he raised his feet up and crossed his legs over the rope, now he was facing up toward the roof of the chamber. Jack shimmied himself along the stretch of rope, making his way over to the other side.

Suddenly Albert froze.

He quickly checked the rope. It seemed intact. He pointed his flashlight across to the boulder on the other side where the rope was attached. It was holding nicely.

"What was that sound?" He was sure he heard some sort of clinking sound, like a piece of metal dropping to the cavern floor.

"Jack is your tether secure?" Albert called out.

Jack checked his tether. It looked to be in order. "It seems so, Albert, why?"

Before Albert could answer, his eyes wandered to the iron ring that held the rope in place. He saw that the rope holding Jack was too much for the ring to support and it was beginning to buckle.

The ring was about to snap!

Albert dove into action. He dropped onto his stomach and grabbed the rope, gripping it as tightly as he could. Emma realized what was happening and joined Albert. Together they grimaced and groaned, determined not to lose their hold.

Sensing something was wrong, Jack quickly, but calmly scurried toward the ledge. Behind him, he heard shrieks and groans as Albert and Emma gripped the rope with all their might and called to Jack to move quickly.

"Hurry, Jack, we can't hold this for much longer...", wailed Emma, her hands burning from the rubbing rope.

Jack reached the other side and climbed up onto the ledge. He unclipped his tether and called back to the others. "Piece of cake, who's next?" he joked.

Emma and Albert sighed with relief as they let go of the rope. It remained attached, still dangling from the ring. Their hands burned, and their hearts raced.

It was a close call for Jack, who took a moment to understand the potential danger he'd just escaped.

"Whoa!" said Jack as he shone his flashlight back towards Emma and Albert, then at the damaged ring.

"Albert, that was quick thinking, buddy. You saved me from a close encounter with some pretty spooky skeletons! Are you both ok?"

"I'm alright," Albert replied, "Glad you didn't lose your sense of humor, Jack!"

Albert and Emma knew it was not going to be safe for either of them to use that same ring to get across the crevice and join Jack.

It was too weak and too damaged.

"Now how will we get across?" asked Emma as she blew on her hands to relieve the burning sensation.

"Ok, so now I get to test *my* knot-tying skills," said Albert as he untied the rope from the damaged ring and began to loop it to the other ring. Once it was secured, Albert took the slack from the rope and tied it to the torch that was securely attached to the wall.

"This ring feels stronger than the last one, but it doesn't hurt to have a backup, just in case".

"Good thinking Albert."

"Emma how about you go first. I'll be here to make sure there are no issues, and I can catch the rope if needed, ok?"

"Oh, thanks Albert." Emma put on her climbing gloves and attached her tether.

"Here goes nothing," she said as she held the rope and lowered herself off the ledge. Emma carefully crossed the crevice to meet Jack.

The second ring seemed to be holding up well, and even though Albert was a little uncertain, he took a deep breath, lowered himself off the ledge and slowly made his way across.

Once they were all safely on the other side, there were hugs, smiles and high-fives all around.

Then, they turned their attention to the next obstacle on their quest. Albert found and lit more torches along the cave walls and they all looked around.

CHAPTER SEVEN

The new platform they found themselves on was very similar to the first, however instead of a small passageway leading into the wall, there was a stone door. The door was very solid and there wasn't any handle.

The three adventurers tried with all their might to push it open, but it didn't budge an inch.

Jack pulled out his tablet and they looked at the clues, hoping for an idea to help them open the door.

Jack pointed to the second clue "Hey, this could be something..."

No handle, no lock, nor hinges to rust.
Balance is the key, find it you must.

"Look guys, do you see those two shelves up there beside the doorway?" asked Jack.

Shining his flashlight up to them, he could make out two wooden planks, each hanging by ropes that disappeared through holes in the rocks above.

"Maybe... we need to balance something on them to open the door?" Emma added, as she shone her flashlight toward one, then the other.

"Yeah, that makes sense, let's look around and see what we can put up there," said Albert as he searched around for something that might work as a weight.

"Over here, look! There's stone blocks piled up between the boulders, let's try one."

He picked up one of the blocks, then reached up and placed it on one of the wooden planks. There was a faint grinding noise and the plank started lowering down toward the ground, but nothing happened to the door.

"Wait!" said Emma, "It says we need *balance* to open the door, so I think we need to add blocks to both sides at the same time."

She walked over to collect another block.

"Albert, can you please remove your block and we'll try adding one to each side at the same time?"

"Sure Emma, great idea!" Albert replied, as he lifted his block off the plank and it slowly rumbled back up to the top again.

Once Emma was standing beside the right platform and Albert beside the left, they each held up a stone block that was roughly the same size.

"Alright Albert, on three we each place our block on the platforms, are you ready?"

"Yep, ready when you are!" Albert replied.

Emma began counting "One... Two... Three, *now*!"

Both Emma and Albert placed their blocks on the platforms at the same time. Now there was a louder rumbling as both platforms lowered a little, and the bottom of the door raised a little.

"Great, that's it!" Emma exclaimed. "Now we just need to keep adding blocks together until the door is open all the way and we can pass through!"

They worked quickly to add blocks to the platforms until the door opened all the way and the platforms, now loaded with stones rested on the floor.

"Great work, guys!" Jack shone his flashlight inside the doorway and led the way.

Soon the three found themselves on yet another ledge, this time inside and toward the top of a very large cavern. The sound of water could be heard, as the echo of small lapping waves bounced off the hard rock walls around them.

There was a faint and eerie blue glow in the distance, and as they stepped carefully toward the edge, the rest of the chamber came into view.

The sight before them was spectacular and all three gasped.

After a few moments of silence, Albert was the first to speak "Tell me I'm not dreaming – that *is* what I think it is, right?"

Emma giggled with excitement, "Aha! We've found it."

"Even in this low light, that sure does look like a Spanish treasure galleon to me," Jack agreed as he pulled out his tablet to snap a photo of their discovery.

Silhouetted against the pale blue glow illuminating the large stone chamber, was the unmistakable shape of a large, wooden sailing ship.

"Now how did *that* get inside a mountain?" Emma asked, curiously.

"Good question Em, we need to get down there and take a closer look. We also need to find out where that light is coming from...

and if there is any treasure on that ship!" replied Jack as he enthusiastically surveyed the cavern.

"How do we get down there?" wondered Albert as he looked around for options.

"Well, it's definitely too far to jump," joked Jack, "perhaps I can rig up some ropes here and we can lower ourselves down this wall."

"Hold that thought," Albert said, as he found and lit yet another torch on the wall, revealing the beginning of a staircase.

It appeared to be chiseled out of the stone wall and headed downward. "I think I've found a much easier way!"

Emma walked over and looked down the stairs. "Brilliant, let's go!"

Jack laughed, "Good find, Albert, definitely quicker than my idea!"

Eager to explore the ship, the team started heading down the rough, rocky stairs, lighting torches along the way.

They reached the bottom and found a small, wooden rowboat tied to the shore and bobbing gently in the water.

Now that they were closer, Jack, Emma and Albert could see that the ship was anchored a short distance from the shore.

Perhaps the most exciting discovery up to this point was that, even though the lettering was a little faded and worn, they could make out the ship's name on her stern.

"JJ! Albert! It's the Invincible. We've found her! Do you think the treasure is still aboard?"

"Well, there's only one way to find out... let's get into this rowboat so we can take a look!"

CHAPTER EIGHT

After untying the small boat, Jack, Emma and Albert climbed aboard and began rowing out toward the large ship.

It was slow going. The boat was barely sea-worthy, but even with the leaks, creaks, barnacles and slime, the crew managed to make it work.

"Over there, Jack, there's a rope ladder hanging down the side." Albert pointed his flashlight toward the ladder, guiding them in.

Once they reached it, they tied the small boat to the ship and climbed up the ladder. Jack led the way followed by Emma and Albert.

The ship rocked ever so slightly in the small cove, and the occasional soft creaking of wood and rigging echoed off the cavern walls as they walked the deck.

"She's certainly lived up to her name. It's all in incredibly good condition, considering how long it has been here," Albert observed, looking around the deck before turning his attention and flashlight up to the rigging. "The sails are pretty tattered, I don't know if she'd still sail like that."

"You're right, it really is amazing," Jack replied in awe, "I'm going to send Mom and Dad an update... they'll be excited to hear about this!"

Jack tried to send a message but there was no signal on his tablet. When that didn't work they tried the walkie-talkie to check-in with Roberto. But they only heard static.

"I'm guessing the walls are too thick to get any signal out, we'll have to figure out a way to make contact," said Jack as he shone his flashlight around the cavern walls.

"In the meantime, though, let's go below deck and see what we can find."

It took about half-an-hour of searching before they located the secure storage room in the lower decks, then about that much time again to find the keys hidden in the captain's cabin.

But when they finally opened the door, what they saw was beyond anything they could have ever imagined.

"Wow! This is unbelievable!" gasped Emma.

"I'll say!" replied Albert in amazement, "Look at all of this gold!"

The room was stacked floor to ceiling with shelves – most of them lined with row after row of solid-gold bars.

There were also several large, rectangular chests, bursting with riches, along with some sparkling statues and interesting artwork that sat neatly on another set of shelves.

"I think we've hit the jackpot!" Jack beamed, as he began opening some of the chests to reveal gold coins, brilliant gems and breathtaking jewels. "How will we get all of this out of here?"

"I was just thinking about that. I have an idea, follow me...," answered Albert.

Albert led the way back up to the open deck of the galleon and then to the bow of the ship where he pointed toward the far wall of the chamber.

"I noticed this before, but we were busy looking for the treasure, so I didn't mention it. That's where the light is coming in, do you see that brighter glow in the water there?"

"Yes, I see it," Emma replied.

"And above it, do you see those beams of wood that seem to be holding the wall up?"

"Yeah, I see that, what does it mean?" asked Jack.

"It looks to me like that may have been an opening once, that's probably how they got the ship in here."

"Ahh, I see, then they built that platform and collapsed some of the rocks down on it to close off this chamber after they had sailed the ship inside."

"Exactly! That's probably what all that gunpowder was for!"

"That makes sense," Emma agreed.

"So, how does that help us get out?" remarked Jack.

"I'm glad you asked! I think that the pirate crew hid the galleon here and planned to come back and get the treasure. They set up the traps and pitfalls to stop anyone else from finding it, or just in case someone stumbled across it. Can you show me the letter again, remember that last clue?"

Jack pulled out his tablet and they all looked at the final clue in the letter.

Light the wick then take cover fast,
A boom and a blast will clear the path,
Then ye shall have the very last laugh.

"Good thinking, Albert! So, if you're correct there must be more gunpowder and a fuse around here that we need to light. The explosion should cause that wall to collapse and re-open the entrance to this cave?" cried Jack, bursting with excitement.

"Right!" replied Albert, "I think they planned to come back and set it all up, so they could just sail her out of here one day."

"Only they never got to come back," frowned Emma.

"Yeah... perhaps we can finish what they started..." said Jack.

Emma thought for a moment, "I think that's what Samuel McDougal would have wanted, that's why he wrote that letter and made the map. Let's do it!"

The three got back into the small boat and rowed over to the artificial wall searching for the fuse. They located it after a short while, along with several barrels of gunpowder that were placed strategically at the base of the wall.

Then the trio found a protected alcove nearby where they could seek shelter.

"I sure hope you're right about this, Albert!" joked Jack as he struck a match on a boulder and then proceeded to light the fuse. *"RUN!"*

"Me, too!" Albert replied and the three of them ran as quickly as their legs could carry them to shelter in the alcove.

A few moments later, a deafening *BOOM* echoed all around the cavern, followed by the sounds of rocks, big and small, splashing into the sea and sinking to the deep bottom below.

Emma was the first to peek her head around the corner, "Look, it worked, it's completely open now!"

Jack patted Albert on the back, "Great thinking! Now, do you have any ideas for how we sail her home?"

Albert was about to reply but was interrupted by a crackle and Roberto's voice came over the walkie-talkie. "Jack, come-in, are you okay? I heard a big explosion!"

"I guess the signal can reach us in here now the cave wall is gone," Albert smiled as he thought out loud.

Jack picked up his walkie-talkie and replied, "Roberto! Yes, we are all fine, we've got quite a story to tell you."

"I'm glad to hear you're alright. Can I be of any assistance?"

Jack grinned as an idea popped into his head, "Actually Roberto, when was the last time you used that boat of yours as a tug-boat? We could use a tow."

"No problem, Jack, Hercules can handle whatever you need. Where are you?"

"Sail into the cave on the eastern side of the island, we'll be ready to weigh anchor when you arrive."

"Ah, I don't think there is a cave on this island you can sail into."

Jack laughed, "Well, there is now!"

By the time the familiar *put-put* of Hercules could be heard, Jack, Emma and Albert were all back aboard the Invincible and were waving down to Roberto who had a look of complete disbelief on his face.

The four worked quickly to secure heavy towing lines and get underway so they could reach port before the sun set for the day.

Along the way Jack messaged his parents to fill them in. Mr. and Mrs. Jones were incredibly proud of the children's discovery and suggested they work with the local maritime history museum to decide how best to preserve their wondrous discovery.

As they pulled into the harbor, Jack and Emma's parents, along with many curious onlookers, newspaper reporters and television crews were waiting to greet them at the dock and be among the first to get a peek at the no-longer-hidden ship.

"What an adventure, I can't wait to do this again!" Jack exclaimed as they all posed for photos in front of the galleon.

Emma and Albert nodded in agreement, and all three let their minds wander about where that next adventure might just be.

THE END

JACK JONES

TITLES IN THIS SERIES

COMING SOON

The Desert Quest   The Mysterious Light
Castle on the Cliff   The Ghost Ship

www.jackjonesclub.com

ABOUT THE AUTHOR

Zander Bingham was born and raised on a boat. It was captured by pirates when he was just 12-years-old. He, along with his family and crew, swam to a nearby island where Zander spent his days imagining swashbuckling adventures on the high seas.

Well, not exactly.

But Zander did love boating adventures as a kid. And he always dreamed of exploring deserted islands and being a real-life castaway. He grew up cruising around Australia, the USA and The Bahamas. He eventually captained his very own sail boat, living aboard and exploring the Adriatic Sea with his wife and two young sons.

His thirst for exploration, his witty sense of humor, and his new-found passion for writing stories to read to his boys at bedtime, led to the creation of Jack Jones; the confident, brave and curious boy adventurer who is always searching for his next escapade.

Made in the USA
Monee, IL
07 March 2020